The Boxcar Children Mysteries

THE CUPCAKE CAPER

created by
GERTRUDE CHANDLER WARNER

Illustrated by Robert Papp

Albert Whitman & Company
Chicago, Illinois

Contents

THE CUPCAKE CAPER

CHAPTER 1

Mama Tova's Secret

"Come on, hurry!" six-year-old Benny
Alden said, tugging his sister Violet's hand,
practically dragging her down the sidewalk.
"Mama Tova just took the cupcakes out of
the oven!"

Until a few months ago, the Aldens'
neighbor Maria Tovanoff, who was known
to everyone as "Mama Tova," only made her
tasty cupcakes just for family and friends. But
the treats were so popular that Mama Tova
decided to open a small shop in Greenfield.

She made only 108 cupcakes every day—nine dozen. They all came from the same recipe, but each cupcake was a little different, because Mama Tova added delicious flavors and wonderfully tasty decorations.

When all the cupcakes sold out, the store closed until the next day!

Ten-year-old Violet asked her brother Benny, "How can you tell the cupcakes are ready?"

"My nose knows," Benny said.

Henry and Jessie, their older siblings, began to laugh.

"Benny's nose is amazing," Fourteen-year-old Henry remarked, ruffling Benny's hair.

"His nose is the eighth wonder of the world. And if Benny smells the cupcakes, we'd better hurry," Jessie said, breaking into a run. "I hope Mama Tova has some left when we get there."

Henry's thick brown hair bounced up and down as he kept pace with his twelve-year -old sister. It wasn't long before they arrived at the front of Sweets, Mama Tova's new cupcake bakery.

"Oh no," Henry said, seeing a long line of people in front of the building. "We'll never get a cupcake today."

"Thirty-one, thirty-two," Benny was busy counting the people in front of them in line. Mama Tova's rule was "only one cupcake per person."

"You're number sixty-four!" Benny told Henry, who breathed a sigh of relief.

"Whew! We got here in time," Jessie said happily.

Benny jumped up and down, clapping his hands and shouting, "Hip! Hip! Hurray! We're going to eat a cupcake today."

Very patiently, the Alden children stood in line waiting for their turn at the cupcake counter.

"I wish we could buy an extra cupcake for Grandfather," Violet said.

"Maybe he can come with us next time," Henry replied. "We could bring Watch on a leash and sit outside at the little tables."

Jessie, Violet, Henry and Benny lived with their grandfather. After their parents died, they ran away and hid in a railroad boxcar in the woods. They heard that their Grandfather Alden was mean. Even though they'd never met him, they were afraid. But when he finally found the children, they discovered he wasn't mean at all. Now the children lived with him, and their boxcar was a clubhouse in the backyard. They even got to bring along the stray dog they found on their adventures, a wire-haired terrier named Watch.

"Hey Jessie. Scoot forward, please," Benny told his sister as the cupcake line moved up a little bit.

Jessie and the others took a few steps closer to the boy in front of them. The sisters knew him from school. His name was Pauly and he was in the class between Jessie and Violet. Pauly had straight dark hair and wore braces.

Just before it was his turn at the counter, Pauly turned to Jessie and said, "Can you believe Mama Tova makes me wait in line?

I mean I am her nephew, after all." Pauly complained. "I liked the way it was before she opened the shop. I could have all the cupcakes I wanted, all the time."

Finally they were almost at the head of the line.

"Next!" called Mrs. Waldman, one of the workers at the shop. It was Pauly's turn to order. With a sigh, he pointed at a chocolate chip cupcake with purple frosting.

"At least she still gives them to me for free," Pauly told the Aldens. He went off to eat his cupcake.

"It's our turn!" Benny announced doing his cheer once again, this time adding, "Hip. Hip. Hurray. A yummy cupcake is on its way!"

"This is the last tray," Mama Tova announced. She carried three dozen cupcakes to the front. The shop was so busy that Mama Tova needed helpers. Mrs. Waldman served the cupcakes and poured cold milk or lemonade. A girl named Alicia, who was Henry's age, rang up orders at the cash register.

"Four cupcakes, please," Henry told Alicia. Each of the Alden children picked out the one they wanted. Benny's had chocolate cookie dough frosting. Jessie's was filled with lemon custard and drizzled with lemon icing. Henry's cupcake had a red cinnamon candy frosting. And Violet picked a purple colored cupcake with blueberry frosting.

"Here you go," Alicia said. Her curly blonde hair was pulled up under a hat with a huge, floppy, red fabric flower in the middle. Her apron was printed with the same flowers. It was the Sweets uniform. Mrs. Waldman and Mama Tova wore flowered aprons and hats, too.

Each table at Sweets had a flowered tablecloth and a vase of fresh flowers on it. Floral pictures of all different kinds hung on the walls around the room. And there were little purple lilies on the wallpaper. Outside there were even more flowers in a beautiful planter box.

"I just love the decorations in here," Violet told Jessie as they found a table. "All of the

flowers make me feel so happy and bright."
She touched one of the petals on the flower
in their table vase. "No matter what season it
is outside, it will always be spring at Sweets,"
Violet said.

"You say that every time we come here,"
Jessie said, laughing.

"I know. I think I should paint a picture of
some flowers for my bedroom wall." Violet
glanced around. "Maybe some like that." She
pointed to a painting of a single pink flower.
"I don't even know what kind of flower that is,
but it's so pretty. I could stare at that picture
all day."

Jessie said, "I'll look it up on the internet
when we get home. At least then you'll know
what you're drawing."

"Thanks, Jessie," Violet said.

The children began to eat their cupcakes.
They were so delicious, no one talked while
they ate. Not even Benny.

When he was done, Benny licked his
fingers and sighed. "I'm so sad it's gone."

"We can come back again soon," Henry

assured Benny, while Jessie handed him a napkin.

"So, how about same time, next week?" Benny asked his brother, eyes wide. "And then we could come the week after that, too."

"And maybe even the one after that," Henry promised.

When all the children were finished, they took their plates and cups to the counter.

"Thanks," Alicia said, taking the dishes.

"Wow, Alicia," Jessie said, "Your necklace is so pretty." Alicia was wearing a gold chain with a large glittery letter *G* hanging from it.

"Thanks," she said again, lightly touching the letter. "It's new."

Just before the Aldens left the shop, Mama Tova came out of the kitchen. She always spent some time in the shop, welcoming her customers. "Hello children," she greeted as she made her way through the crowd. "How'd you like the cupcakes?"

"I could have eaten all 108 of them by myself," Benny exclaimed, patting his stomach. "Why are your cupcakes so good?"

Mama Tova chuckled. "It's because of my secret ingredient. I put it in all the cupcakes I make."

"Oh, will you tell me what it is?" Benny asked. "Please?"

Mama Tova ruffled Benny's shiny dark brown hair. "Sorry, Benny. It's an old family recipe. I can't tell anyone, ever. But I will tell you this…" She smiled, then said, "I keep the secret ingredient right here at the shop, underneath the flower."

Jessie, Henry, Violet and Benny looked around the shop at all the different flowers. There were flowers everywhere!

Mama Tova winked. Then they all laughed together.

CHAPTER 2

A Cupcake Contest

The bell to the cupcake shop's door jingled. A tall man entered the store. He wore a suit and his dark hair and mustache were very neatly trimmed.

Mama Tova looked up. "Oh, Mr. Kandinsky. You're back."

"Good day, Mama Tova," Mr. Kandinsky said. "I hope you have had time to think about my offer." Mr. Kandinsky ran one hand over his tie, smoothing the silk flat against his chest.

Jessie wondered what the man wanted. "No thank you, Mr. Kandinsky," Mama Tova said. "I cannot possibly sell you my cupcake recipe."

Benny's eyes grew wide. "Why do you want her recipe?" he asked Mr. Kandinsky. "It's a very big secret. She won't even tell *me* what the mystery ingredient is!"

"I am the owner of BakeMart," Mr. Kandinsky said. "We are Greenfield's biggest bread factory."

"I went there on a school field trip!" Henry exclaimed. "You make all kinds of bread for the grocery stores and restaurants around town." He added, "It's a huge factory. All silver and shiny and clean. Impressive."

"Why, thank you," Mr. Kandinsky said. "Our business is doing so well that it's time for BakeMart to grow. We want to make something new." He looked around the shop. "We think Mama Tova's cupcakes would be a perfect BakeMart product."

At that, Mama Tova shook her head. "No, no," she said. "I like making my cupcakes unique and special. I don't want my cupcakes in every grocery store and restaurant."

"You are thinking small," Mr. Kandinsky said. "From the moment I tasted one of your treats, I knew that you and your cupcakes could be big! Kids everywhere would be eating them fresh out of the package. We could even put your face on the wrapper."

He took a thick stack of papers out of his jacket pocket and set them on a nearby table. "Here is a contract. You'll see I am willing to give you a lot of money for the recipe with your secret ingredient."

"No," Mama Tova said firmly. She picked up the contract and handed it back to Mr. Kandinsky. "I will not give you my recipe. It's a family secret. And I won't sell it for all the money in the world. If you want a cupcake, come by tomorrow and get in line with everyone else."

And with that, Mama Tova pointed to the shop door. "Good day to you, Mr. Kandinsky," she said clearly.

Mr. Kandinsky tucked the contract back

into his pocket. "You'll be sorry, Mama Tova," he said. "BakeMart will get a recipe better than yours. People will buy our cupcakes at every shop in town and your little store here will have to close! You'll have no more business."

"That's not true!" Benny said, taking a big step forward. "Mama Tova will always have the best cupcakes. Forever!"

Mr. Kandinsky turned around and looked straight at Benny. "That sounds like a challenge," he said. He pressed his lips together for a moment, looking thoughtful. "Thanks to this boy, I have a brilliant idea."

Benny stepped back. He didn't mean to give the man any ideas.

"I propose we have a contest!" Mr. Kandinsky announced. Then he called out to the crowded room. "Attention everyone! BakeMart will be having a cupcake bake-off. Bring your best cupcakes and the recipe. The prize is a thousand dollars and BakeMart will make the winning cupcakes." He smiled so widely that the edges of his mustache rose up a little. "The contest will be held at the BakeMart factory next Saturday at noon. See you all there!"

Mr. Kandinsky left the shop, slamming the door behind him.

"Oh no," Benny groaned. "A cupcake contest." He covered his head with his arms. "It's all my fault."

"No it's not, Benny," Henry told his brother. "You didn't do anything wrong."

"But what if he gets a really good cupcake? And then Mama Tova will have to close her store because everyone is eating BakeMart cupcakes!" Benny peeked up at Henry through his arms.

Jessie leaned in and put an arm around Benny. Violet shook her head.

"Don't worry, Benny," Jessie said. "Can you imagine anyone on earth with a better cupcake than Mama Tova? You've eaten a whole lot of cupcakes, right? Are there any more delicious?"

Benny popped his head up. "You're right! Her cupcakes are the best ever!"

Mama Tova didn't look worried at all when the children said goodbye. In fact she said, "I wish Mr. Kandinsky luck. The Tova family recipe has won every cupcake contest for years. The Tovas have baked for kings and queens and princes." Mama Tova straightened her apron.

"You know, I do feel like a king when I eat one of your cupcakes," Benny told Mama Tova. "Know what else?"

"What?" she asked.

"I'm glad you are going to keep the secret ingredient a secret." Benny smiled big at Mama Tova and she smiled right back at him.

CHAPTER 3

A Ghost in Greenfield?

After dinner that night Jessie took Watch for a walk. They were walking towards the park when Watch began to bark. "What's going on, boy?" she asked the dog, trying to calm him down.

A woman was coming through the park carrying a pink cake box. She walked quickly. She looked odd because her skin, clothes, and hair were completely white.

That woman looks like a ghost! Jessie thought, even though she did not believe in ghosts.

She believed that there was an explanation for everything.

Watch barked again, then pulled his leash free from Jessie's hand.

"Oh no!" Jessie called, rushing after the dog. "Stop! Watch! Stop!"

But it was too late. Watch ran over to the woman, and in his excitement he knocked her to the ground.

"Oh dear," the woman said, scrambling to get up and gather her pink box, which had fallen.

The "ghost" woman turned out to be Mrs. Waldman from Sweets. She was covered head to toe in baking flour!

"I'm so sorry about Watch," Jessie told her. "Here, let me help you up."

"My cupcakes?" Mrs. Waldman asked, anxiously pointing at the box. "Are they all right?"

Jessie snatched the box up before Watch could get to it. She peeked inside. There were four cupcakes, each one uniquely decorated. They looked just like Mama Tova's cupcakes!

"They're fine," Jessie said, handing the box back to Mrs. Waldman. "The frosting smeared a little bit, but they are still very pretty."

"Oh, thank goodness!" Mrs. Waldman said, brushing some of the flour off her dress. It puffed around her in a white cloud.

Jessie coughed. "Wow! That's a lot of flour!" she exclaimed.

Mrs. Waldman looked down at herself. "Yes, it was a very long, messy day at work. I'm headed home now to clean up." She shook off a bit more of the flour. And then, very quickly, she hurried away.

* * *

The next morning the Aldens' home telephone rang and Grandfather answered it. Who could be calling so early? Jessie wondered. She heard Grandfather say, "Oh, no!"

"Who was that?" Jessie asked when Grandfather had hung up the phone.

"That was Mama Tova. Something terrible

happened at the shop last night," he said.

Jessie gasped. Violet hurried over to hear more.

"Someone broke into Sweets and made a mess last night," Grandfather said. "Mama Tova said the shop is a mess! There's baking flour everywhere."

"That is strange," Henry said.

"We should go to Sweets," Violet suggested. "Maybe we can help clean up."

"Good idea," Grandfather said. "We can bring some brooms and dustpans. And a mop and a bucket."

The Aldens loaded the cleaning supplies into Grandfather's car. Watch jumped in the back seat with them.

At Sweets, Jessie tied Watch outside near Mama Tova's brightly colored flower boxes. Then the children went inside to see the damage.

Henry shook his head. "This is awful," he said to Jessie.

It looked like someone had turned the entire shop upside down. The tables were

knocked on their sides, and the flower vases had spilled. Some of the paintings were on the floor. A light dusting of white flour covered everything.

"Thank you so much for coming," Mama Tova said to the Alden children and Grandfather. "I don't know who possibly could have done this, but the police are investigating."

She pointed to a police officer standing in the corner, talking to Mrs. Waldman. "That's Officer Montag," Mama Tova explained. "She's interviewing everyone who might have seen something suspicious."

"I wonder if Mrs. Waldman told her about the flour," Jessie said, glancing over at the police officer.

"Mrs. Waldman?" Mama Tova said. "Flour? What do you mean?"

"I saw Mrs. Waldman last night," Jessie said. "She was covered with flour."

"Does Mrs. Waldman ever do any of the baking?" Henry asked Mama Tova.

"No," Mama Tova said. "Because of the

secret ingredient, I do it all."

"Hmm," Jessie said as she pulled a black spiral notebook out of her patchwork purse. Jessie liked to write things down so she could think about them later. "Do you have any idea who might want to mess up Sweets?" she asked Mama Tova.

"I really don't know." Mama Tova shook her head and sighed. "Officer Montag thinks that the person who did this must have been looking for something in particular. That's why everything is torn apart."

"Were they looking for money?" Benny asked.

"I don't think so, because none of it is gone," Mama Tova said. "I've checked all around the shop and as far as I can tell, nothing is missing."

"Are you sure?" Henry asked.

"All that happened here was that someone made a mess," Mama Tova said. "I wish I knew who would do this and why."

"Maybe we can help," Henry suggested. "We are good at solving mysteries."

"I'd be grateful," Mama Tova said. Then she went to speak to the police officer.

The Aldens walked over to a quiet corner of the shop. Jessie opened a clean page in her notebook and wrote SUSPECTS at the top. Tapping her pencil, Jessie asked the others, "Any ideas?"

Violet spoke up. "I don't know *who* would mess up the shop but I think I know *why*."

"Go on," Henry said. "Explain."

Violet pointed all around the shop. "Remember when Mama Tova told us yesterday that she hid the secret ingredient for her cupcakes under the flower?"

"Someone must have overheard," Henry said. "And they messed up all the shop's flowers looking for the recipe."

"I bet you're both right!" Jessie said. "Maybe Mr. Kandinsky should be our first suspect." She wrote down the BakeMart owner's name in her notebook.

"Is it because Mr. Kandinsky wants the cupcake recipe and Mama Tova won't sell it to him? So maybe he tried to steal it?" Benny asked.

"That's right, Benny," Henry said.

"And then there is Mrs. Waldman and the mysterious flour," Violet said. She remembered Jessie's story. "I think she should be the next suspect."

"Mrs. Waldman also had four of Mama Tova's cupcakes in a box, but nobody is ever allowed to buy more than one cupcake at a time at Sweets. Or take them home. That makes Mrs. Waldman even more suspicious!" Jessie said. She wrote down Mrs. Waldman's name.

"Should we tell Officer Montag what we know?" Benny asked.

"Not yet," Henry said. "So far we aren't really sure about anything."

"We could talk to Mrs. Waldman right now," Benny said. "We just saw her talking to the police."

But when the children looked around, Mrs. Waldman was gone. She had left the shop.

"We'll have to talk to her tomorrow,

I guess," Violet said.

Jessie agreed, shutting her notebook. "We shouldn't tell the police anything until we have more clues about who is trying to steal the recipe."

"We need to solve this mystery before the thief steals the recipe for real," Benny declared.

CHAPTER 4

The Clue in the Flowers

At lunch the next day, Grandfather had an announcement to make. "Mama Tova called a little while ago. She wants us all to come to Sweets before the store opens."

"Did something else bad happen?" Benny asked.

"No," Grandfather said. "She wants to thank you for helping her clean up yesterday, Mama Tova is going to make some special cupcakes."

Benny jumped up and ran out the door. A

minute later, he stuck his head back inside. "Aren't you coming?" he asked his brother and sisters.

Henry laughed. "We're coming, Benny." He stood and began clearing the table. "We have plenty of time to clean up from our lunch and still get to the store when it opens."

"Oh. Right." Benny grabbed as many dishes as he could carry from the table and quickly took them in one huge stack to the sink. When he came back for a second load, Violet had to grab her carrot sticks before her plate disappeared.

"Okay," Benny said, returning to the table. "Dishes are in the sink." He looked at his family. "Can we wash them later? After the cupcakes?" He rubbed his belly. "My stomach can hear the cupcakes calling me."

Everyone giggled.

"Grab your jackets," Grandfather told the children. "You can ride your bikes over. I'll wash up and meet you there."

Benny gave Grandfather a big hug. "Thanks!" he said, and rushed out of the house.

Jessie grabbed her notebook on her way out the door. She hoped Mrs. Waldman would be at the cupcake shop too. There were some questions she wanted to ask.

* * *

"Why is there dirt all over the sidewalk?" Jessie asked Violet as they parked their bikes in front of Sweets. The pavement was covered with crumpled flowers and dirt.

Violet stared at the mess. "It can't be!" she cried. "It looks like someone dug up Mama Tova's beautiful flower boxes."

"Oh no!" Benny exclaimed, getting off his bicycle. "It *is* another mess!"

Alicia came out of the store just then. She was holding a shovel. "Oh," she said when she saw the Aldens, "What are you doing here?"

Benny said, "Mama Tova invited us to a little thank-you party she was having at the shop today. She said to come before the store opened."

"I didn't realize Mama Tova was coming to the store early today," Alicia said, looking down at the dirt. "I was walking by the shop, on my way to the bookstore when I saw this big mess. So I went inside and got a shovel so I could start cleaning it up for her."

Henry said, "We can help, too."

"Mama Tova should know what happened." Jessie said. "I think we need to go call her." She and Violet went to use the phone. Benny and Henry and Alicia started to pick up the flowers, hoping some of them could be saved.

"I'm glad Grandfather taught us how to plant flowers," Benny said, looking at a wilted marigold's roots.

Henry smiled. "Maybe you'll be a gardener when you grow up."

"I don't think so," Benny said, shaking his head. "I would rather be a chef. I'll make steak, and baked potatoes, and delicious desserts, and then *more* steak!"

"Mmmm. I'll come eat at your restaurant every day," Henry said, grinning at his brother.

Mama Tova arrived with Jessie and Violet. She was carrying a bag of soil and a watering can.

Grandfather pulled up in his car at the same time.

"The girls just told me about the mess," Mama Tova said. "I brought some supplies." She set down the soil and picked up one of her torn plants. "So sad," she said, inspecting it closely. "I don't understand why someone would dig up my flowers!"

"I'll go fill the watering can," Alicia said, and rushed off behind the building.

"We think we know why someone would dig them up," Jessie said, taking out her notebook.

"Remember when you told us that the secret ingredient for the cupcakes was under the flower?" Henry reminded Mama Tova. "We think someone overheard you and now they're searching for your recipe."

"They are looking under all your flowers!" Benny added.

"Flowers?" Mama Tova said. Closing her

eyes, she shook her head. "I don't understand. And what does this have to do with the mess from yesterday?"

"I know!" Jessie exclaimed. "Someone heard you say where the secret is kept, but they didn't know if you meant f-l-o-w-e-r, like plants and decorations, or f-l-o-u-r, as in the white powdery stuff for baking."

"Flower or flour?" Mama Tova wondered aloud. "Well then, now I see why someone tore up all my decorations and spilled my baking flour everywhere, too. Goodness me, I can't let them get my family recipe! What am I going to do?"

"We are here to help," Benny said. "We'll clean up today and also to find out who did this."

"Thank you," Mama Tova replied with a sigh as they all set to work replanting the flowers. Alicia came back with the water and then, using her shovel, prepared the planter. She put in new soil while Jessie and Violet dug little holes for the plants.

"There are a few plants missing,"

Grandfather said, counting the holes and the healthy plants. "Unfortunately some flowers lost all their petals. But don't worry, Mama Tova," he said, putting his arm around her. "I've got plenty of flowers in my own garden. I can bring some here." Grandfather left for a few minutes while the children worked on cleaning off the sidewalk. He returned with some beautiful daisies and snapdragons.

After Alicia and the Alden children were finished planting and watering, Mama Tova apologized to them. "I am so sorry. With the flower mess, I don't have time to make a special cupcake party for you children today. I need to get ready to open the store for customers now."

"No party?" Benny said in a sad voice. "But we are already here. Maybe we could wait until the cupcakes are ready."

"Tell you what," Henry said to Benny, "We can come back for cupcakes another day. Today, let's go have an ice cream cone instead."

At that, Benny's face lit up. "Really?" he

asked his brother.

Henry looked to Grandfather for approval. Grandfather said, "A terrific idea."

Alicia and Mama Tova went inside to get Sweets ready for business. The Aldens walked across the street to the ice cream parlor and went inside.

Pauly Tova was sitting at a table near the door. He was eating a chocolate sundae.

While Grandfather ordered ice cream cones, the Aldens talked to Mama Tova's nephew.

Pauly pointed at his watch. "Sweets doesn't open for a while. I couldn't wait that long to get a treat."

"Did you hear about the mess over at Sweets?" Benny asked.

"Sure," Pauly said. "I went there yesterday as soon as I heard, but you had already been there. The whole place was cleaned up."

"I didn't mean that mess," Benny replied. "I meant today's mess."

"What are you talking about?" Pauly said.

"Didn't you see what happened to the flower

planter boxes?" Jessie asked. Pauly was sitting at the window right across from Sweets.

"Huh?" Pauly looked out the window. "What happened?"

Violet explained what had happened.

"I can't believe it!" Pauly exclaimed. "I've been here for a while and never saw anything. I must have been concentrating on my ice cream."

Pauly took a long look at his aunt's shop and then told the Aldens, "You know, some day I'm going to take over Sweets. The secret recipe has to go to someone in the family. And I am family." He paused then added, "When I get that recipe, I won't hang onto it like Aunt Tova. I'll sell it for sure to the person who offers the most money. I'm going to drive a fancy car and have so many baseball cards that they will fill a whole room in my mansion." Pauly pulled a small stack of baseball cards out from his pocket. "I already have a few, but I am going to have way, way more!"

"Really? You want more baseball cards?"

Benny asked, looking at the pile. "But that's not what Mama Tova wants. I don't think she likes baseball."

While Pauly was showing the cards to Henry, Jessie saw that his fingernails were very dirty. But as soon as Pauly noticed her looking at his fingers, he dropped the cards and slid his hands under the table.

"All my aunt wants to do is to make cupcakes! Her little store is too small to ever make her rich!" Pauly told Benny. "But someday there will be Pauly Tova cupcakes in every store all over Greenfield. You'll see."

Just then Grandfather came over with the ice cream cones.

"I better go over and make sure Aunt Tova is okay," Pauly said. "Maybe I can help get the shop ready to open." Pauly took his trash to the can and waved goodbye.

"Did you see his fingernails?" Jessie asked the others. "I really think we need to put Pauly on the suspect list. Not only does he want to sell the recipe, but he had a lot of brown stuff under his finger nails. Maybe it's dirt from the planter box!"

"Or it might just be chocolate from his sundae," Violet noted.

Henry said, "It's impossible to tell."

"Well, then," Jessie said, pulling out her notebook and clicking open her pen, "until we are sure what it is, Pauly Tova has just become Suspect Number Three."

CHAPTER 5

A Visit to BakeMart

The next afternoon, Grandfather drove the children to the BakeMart factory. When he pulled up in front, he told them, "I have some errands to run nearby. I'll be back for you children in half an hour."

"Perfect," Jessie said. "That's just long enough for us to see who is signed up for Saturday's contest."

"We're looking for more suspects," Benny told Grandfather, before opening his door and popping out of the car.

"You really think that whoever is doing this to Mama Tova's store has already entered the contest?" Violet asked Jessie.

"Maybe," Jessie told her. "Today is the last day to sign up. Even if they don't have the recipe yet, the thief knows that Mama Tova's recipe would win for sure. I think they won't give up looking for it until they have that recipe!"

BakeMart was a large concrete and brick building. "Wow!" Benny said, counting the rows of windows. "Six floors! This place is huge."

"Yes, it is," Grandfather said, as the children got ready to go inside. To Benny he said, "Be careful. Be polite. And don't get lost, or in trouble."

"I've been here before," Henry said. He reminded Grandfather of the school trip he'd taken. "I know my way around." Henry assured Grandfather that he'd take care of the others.

"All right. Thirty minutes," Grandfather repeated. "Then meet me right here." There was a sign that said *BakeMart—Breads*.

"We'll be here," Henry told him, taking Benny's hand in his, ready to walk in the front door of the factory.

When Grandfather drove off, Violet pointed at the sign. "Look at that. There's just enough room at the end of the sign to add 'And Cupcakes,'" she said.

"Mr. Kandinsky can make all the cupcakes he likes," Benny said, stomping his foot. "But not Mama Tova's." There was a small room at the side of the long main building. There was a poster and balloons to show where to sign up for the contest.

Benny pulled free from Henry and led the way, going into the room first. "I'll get that list!" Benny headed toward the counter but on his way he stopped and looked around the room. On long tables were samples of all the products BakeMart made. Benny's nose led him to a tray of pecan bread slices. He snatched one up and was about to eat the whole piece all at once.

"Slow down," Jessie said. "Remember,

Grandfather said to be polite."

Benny looked down at his treat and took a small bite instead. "Mmmm."

A girl in a BakeMart uniform came over and handed each of the Aldens a card and a mini pencil. "Please fill out these comment cards. Here at BakeMart, we like to hear what our customers think."

Benny immediately gobbled up the rest of the pecan bread. "How do you spell 'Yummy'?" he asked Henry.

"We don't have time to sample everything," Henry told Benny. "Did you already forget why we are here?"

"I didn't forget, but I also didn't know there'd be snacks!" Benny looked at the trays all around him and said, "Maybe we can eat while we look at the contest list?"

"Sorry." Jessie shook her head. "Let's do what we need to first. If there is extra time, we can try a few things."

They walked over the counter to talk to the girl in the BakeMart uniform. She was brunette, with her hair in a pigtail. Her

nametag said *Gretchen*.

Violet noticed that she was wearing a gold letter *A* on a chain around her neck.

She pointed out the necklace to Jessie, saying quietly, "Isn't that odd? Her name starts with a *G*."

"Maybe it's for her mom's name or a nickname," Jessie whispered.

"I swear I've seen one kind of like it before." Violet shook her head to clear her thoughts. "But I can't remember where."

Jessie decided to see if she could help Violet remember. She went over to Gretchen and said, "I think your necklace is terrific. I was wondering where you got it."

Gretchen put her hand on the glittery letter and smiled. "It was a present for my birthday. It's called a 'Best Friends' necklace. They are really popular."

"I like it," Violet said.

"We can find out where to buy one if you want," Jessie told her sister.

"I don't think we need to." Violet shrugged. "There's just something about it pulling at me, but my mind's blank. Oh well. Not important, I guess."

"We should really get a look at that list," Henry told the others.

Benny asked Gretchen, "Can we see who has signed up for the BakeMart Cupcake Contest?"

Gretchen took a list out of a drawer. She looked down at Benny and asked, "Are you signing up?" She held out a pen.

"No," Benny said. "I don't make cupcakes. I just eat them."

Gretchen put the list back away. "Mr. Kandinsky told me that I can only show people the list if they are going to sign up. It's a contest rule."

Henry had an idea. He spoke up. "But Benny wants to be a chef when he grows up. Right, Benny?"

Benny nodded. "Yes, I do."

"This is his first contest." Jessie said. "We are going to write his name down on the list."

"Are you sure?" Gretchen asked. She had one hand on the drawer with the list, while looking sideways at Benny. "You said you weren't signing up. Now your brother and sisters say you are. What's going on?"

"I was confused," Benny told her. "All the treats around here… I can't think when I am surrounded by so much bread! It's like kryptonite. Of course I am going to enter the contest." He gave Gretchen a very big smile. She could see where he'd lost his front tooth. Gretchen pulled the list back out.

"Put your name here," she said. She pointed at an empty line.

Henry quickly read over the other names. Benny was nineteenth on the list. There were too many contestants and not enough time to study every name. But he saw Gretchen's name on the list. "You're entering the contest?" Henry asked.

"Of course," Gretchen said. "A thousand dollars would be a big boost to my college fund."

She handed Benny a ballpoint pen. "You can sign up, but I wouldn't bother if I were you. I know I'm going to win. I've got a great plan. So you shouldn't waste your time."

"But maybe I'll make a terrific cupcake," Benny said as he carefully wrote his name. Jessie and Violet peered over his shoulder, looking at the other names.

"Maybe," Gretchen said. "But I am certain that the top prize will be mine!"

When they moved away from the desk, Violet told Jessie, "I think you should put Gretchen on the suspect list, okay?"

"Why?" Jessie asked, opening her notebook to the right page. "Is this about the necklace?"

"No," Violet said, "I think she's suspicious because Gretchen said she has a plan to win the contest."

"Maybe stealing the recipe is her plan?" Jessie asked. "Then again, how could she know where it is hidden? She wasn't at Sweets when Mama Tova told us it was under the flower."

"It's possible that someone who was there told Gretchen about it," Henry said.

"And then Gretchen made her plan?"

Benny asked.

Violet shrugged. "Maybe."

"Speaking of recipes," Henry said. "We are going to need one for Benny to use." He looked over at Benny, who was quickly finishing samples from the last tray in the room. In three minutes, he'd managed to taste every single kind of bread!

"It was a great idea to enter Benny in the contest," Jessie said. "Now we have a real reason to be there. It'll make checking things out a lot easier."

"Yeah," Violet said. "But where are we going to find a cupcake recipe that Benny can make?"

"I'll find one," Jessie said. "There are plenty of good recipes on the internet."

Just before the children left the BakeMart shop Mr. Kandinsky came in.

"The contest is now officially closed," he told Gretchen with a twitch of his moustache. "There can be no more entries." Mr. Kandinsky took the list from her, gave it a quick glance, folded it and slipped the page into his pocket. "I look forward to tasting your cupcake on Saturday, Gretchen."

She smiled at him. "It'll be the best one there, I'm positive."

"I entered the contest, too!" Benny said, rushing up to Mr. Kandinsky. "I'm so excited."

"What kind of cupcake are you making?" Mr. Kandinsky asked, bending down to talk to Benny.

Benny looked at Jessie, who looked at Henry. They all turned to Violet.

"Chocolate Surprise," Violet said. She'd made up the flavor on the spot.

"The cake part will be chocolate, but there will also be a surprise inside!" Benny said, clapping his hands at the idea.

"Sounds delicious," Mr. Kandinsky said. "I'll look forward to tasting your entry too." He stood up and prepared to leave the room. "Mama Tova better learn to make something else, because soon, my cupcakes will be the best sellers in town!"

Back in the car, Jessie asked Grandfather

if they could head over to Mama Tova's shop instead of going straight home. "The contest is only two days away," she told him. "We need to come up with a plan!"

CHAPTER 6

Questions for Mrs. Waldman

When Grandfather dropped off the Aldens at Sweets, Alicia, Mrs. Waldman, and Mama Tova were busy getting ready for the day's business.

Outside the store, on the sidewalk near the newly planted flowers, Jessie took out her notebook. "I think we should review our suspects and then come up with a plan to stop this thief."

"Our first suspect is Mr. Kandinsky," Henry said.

"He wants an excellent cupcake for his factory," Violet said. "But I don't really think he's the one trying to take the recipe. If he was going to steal the recipe, he wouldn't need to have a cupcake contest."

"I see your point." Henry replied. "Mr. Kandinsky isn't entering any cupcakes in the contest himself."

"Sounds like he's not a suspect anymore." Jessie drew a line through Mr. Kandinsky's name as Henry asked, "Who's next?"

"Mrs. Waldman," Jessie said. "It's still very suspicious that she had flour all over her when I saw her that night. Maybe we'll understand it a bit better after we talk to her about it."

Mrs. Waldman was standing near the cash register in the shop.

"Excuse me," Jessie said as they all approached. "You know how we're helping Mama Tova figure out what happened here at the shop?"

"Yes, she told me. How can I help?" Mrs. Waldman asked. She was dressed for work. The flower on her hat bounced a little each time she spoke.

"Jessie saw you covered in flour the other night," said Henry. "We were wondering why."

"Oh, that," Mrs. Waldman said with a smile. "It was my wedding anniversary that night and I wanted to bring my husband some cupcakes as a surprise."

"But Jessie said that you were carrying a box of Mama Tova's cupcakes," Benny added. "Her rules say that no one is allowed to take cupcakes home."

"Those weren't Mama Tova's cupcakes. They were mine." Mrs. Waldman laughed.

"They looked just like Mama Tova's," Jessie remarked. "I peeked in the box."

"Well, that's quite a compliment!" Mrs. Waldman smiled. "Mama Tova taught me how to decorate them. I practice all the time. I can finally get my cupcakes to look like hers, but sadly, they don't taste quite as good. No one will ever make cupcakes as wonderful as Mama Tova!"

Mrs. Waldman led the children into the

kitchen. "I was all set to make the cupcakes from my own recipe, of course, and I ran out of flour." She pointed up to a high shelf. "The extra bags are kept up there."

Benny raised his eyes and said, "It's very high up. Do you have a ladder?"

"I couldn't find one," Mrs. Waldman said. "So I stood on these crates."

There were some wooden boxes beneath the shelves with the words *Woosterville Sasparilla* on them.

Mrs. Waldman stepped onto the crate, saying, "I climbed on top and reached up to the shelf and—"

"The bag of flour fell on you!" Jessie exclaimed as she figured out what had happened.

"Exactly!" Mrs. Waldman said. "I was so upset. I was already running late and now, I had a big mess to clean up. I decided to make the cupcakes first and then sweep up."

She went on. "Lucky for me, Alicia was still at work. She knew I was nervous about getting home before my husband did, I had told her that I wanted everything to be set up when he walked in. Alicia said she had a party to go to, but it wasn't until later. So she said that she'd take care of cleaning up as an anniversary present to me. That girl is an absolute sweetheart."

Mrs. Waldman climbed down off the crate. "I packed up the cupcakes," Mrs. Waldman said, "and I hurried home. That's when I saw you." She pointed at Jessie.

It was Benny's turn. He got onto the crate, but instead of stepping off nicely like Mrs. Waldman, Benny jumped high, arms spread like a superhero. "Wheee!" he cried out as he landed. Then Benny said, "Cross her off, Jessie. Her story makes sense. I declare that Mrs. Waldman is no longer a suspect!"

Jessie put a line through Mrs. Waldman's name.

"Whew," Mrs. Waldman said with a grin. "I hadn't realized I was even on a list, but I'm thrilled to be cleared." She glanced around and saw Mama Tova scurrying about the shop putting flower vases on the tables. Mrs. Waldman said, "I better go. Mama Tova needs my help."

Mrs. Waldman left the kitchen.

Jessie checked her suspects list. She said, "Well, now there are only two suspects left: Pauly and Gretchen."

"Pauly is more suspicious than Gretch—" Henry began, as Mama Tova came into the kitchen. She closed the door behind her and then shut a long black privacy curtain over the kitchen window.

"Everyone must leave the kitchen. Now," Mama Tova told the children.

"Why? What's going on?" Benny asked, taking one last leap from the wooden crate.

"If I don't get the cupcakes made soon, I won't be able to serve my customers today." She shook her head in amazement. "I can't believe it, but there's already a line forming in front of the shop!"

"Already?" Jessie asked. "The shop doesn't open for at least another hour."

"Wow!" Violet said. "The line is starting

earlier and earlier every day. I remember when it was good enough to get here fifteen minutes before opening. Now you have to come a whole hour early!"

"By next week, we might need to bring sleeping bags and stay all night," Benny said, giggling.

"Crazy, isn't it?" Mama Tova said, as she scurried around the kitchen, gathering bowls and measuring spoons. "I feel like a star. This is a dream come true for me. A busy shop. People waiting outside to buy my cupcakes!" She suddenly stopped hustling and sighed. "I just never imagined that someone would be trying to steal my recipe. That's the bad part of my success."

Benny rushed over and gave Mama Tova a hug. "Don't worry," he told her.

"But how can I not?" Mama Tova asked, clearly worried. "I'm so nervous. What will happen to my shop if someone succeeds in stealing the recipe? I would lose my customers, just like Mr. Kandinsky threatened. Then all my dreams would be shattered."

"Hang on! I got it!" Henry exclaimed.

He looked around the kitchen with excitement. "Jessie said we need a plan. And I just figured out what to do. I know how we can stop the thief."

CHAPTER 7

Setting the Trap

The next day, Mama Tova's shop was crowded as usual.

"Don't say anything yet," Henry whispered. Benny, Violet, and Jessie were sitting at a small table in the center of the room, waiting for their cue. Henry was at the next table. He had a plan.

"I want there to be lots of people in the shop when Mama Tova comes over to talk to us," Henry told Jessie.

"You mean just like the day we were here

and she said that the recipe was under the flower?" Violet said.

Henry kept an eye on the door. "Yes," he replied. "Just like that. I am hoping that the same person who heard Mama Tova that day will hear her now."

The little bell on the door chimed and three more people squeezed into the shop. It was so packed that it was hard to move around and the tables were full.

"I think there are more people here now than the other day," Jessie told Henry. "Maybe you should start."

Henry agreed. "Okay. When I stand up, that's the cue for action. Mama Tova will come out of the kitchen, and then you start talking to her. Got it?"

"We got it the first million times you explained," Benny told his brother.

"Sorry," Henry said. "I'm just a little nervous. It's my idea after all. I want this to work."

"It will," Violet said. "It's a good plan, Henry."

Jessie noticed that a few customers were taking their dishes over to Alicia, ready to leave the shop. "You'd better get rolling."

Henry stood up and yawned.

Mama Tova immediately came out of the kitchen. She'd been waiting there, watching Henry. She greeted the other customers as she slowly made her way around the shop. Henry had told her not to come straight over to them. She had to act the same way she did every day.

"How was your cupcake?" she asked a small boy. She smiled at him and moved closer to the table where Jessie and Violet were sitting with Benny.

"And how are you today?" she asked Benny.

"I'm terrific," Benny said. The Aldens had lined up early to come inside. Mama Tova had offered to sneak them in, but they'd refused. They had to make sure it looked like business as usual in the shop.

"Why haven't you eaten your cupcake yet?" Mama Tova asked Benny.

Everyone else had finished their treat. But

not Benny. He kept looking at his, turning it around and around in his hand, smelling the chocolate cake part.

"I'm trying to decide the best way to eat it," Benny explained to Mama Tova. "I could lick off the frosting and then eat the cake part alone."

"That sounds like a good approach," Jessie said.

"Or," Benny went on, "I could peel off the paper and eat it from the bottom up."

"Cake first, icing last," Violet licked her lips. "That's the way I like to go."

"Or," Benny kept going, "I could jump in from the side and make certain that every bite has both cake and frosting."

"I see your problem," Mama Tova said with a laugh. "How are you ever going to decide?"

Benny shook his head. "I just don't know…"

Henry had told his brother and sisters to start the conversation before he stepped forward. It was his turn now.

"Mama Tova," Henry said in a loud voice, much louder than his normal tone.

"Yes?" Mama Tova turned to look at him, just like they'd practiced.

"Your cupcakes are so delicious!" Henry was talking very clearly, so anyone nearby could listen in if they wanted to. "Won't you please tell us the secret ingredient?"

"I just can't do that!" Mama Tova said. "The recipe has been in my family for centuries. But," she paused and then leaned in towards Henry, as if she was going to tell him a secret. "I'll give you a clue—the recipe is hidden under the flower!"

It was the same thing she'd told them before.

The children looked at all the decorations and laughed. Just like they'd also done before. But this time, Mama Tova added, "I have flowers here in the shop and in the window box. But I also have a whole garden in the back."

"Hmm," Henry said. "Sounds like you have a lot of good places to hide the recipe!"

"Ah yes," Mama Tova said. "My secret cupcake recipe is locked in a very special box. It is hidden away next to a wooden bench. Under a flower. Where no one will ever find it."

Mama Tova gave Henry a big wink and returned to the kitchen to finish frosting the final tray of that day's cupcakes.

Henry, Jessie, and Violet hoped the thief had heard the conversation. As for Benny, he finally started eating his cupcake in tiny little bites, from the top down, enjoying every last taste.

*   *   *

That evening the children held a meeting in the boxcar to discuss the recipe trap.

"The fake recipe is locked in a little tin box. We did a good job hiding it," Violet said. "We hid it beneath a pot of daisies, right behind the bakery."

"Henry found the best location," Benny said, grinning at his brother.

"Thanks," Henry said. "I wanted to make

sure the recipe was waiting exactly where Mama Tova described. It had to be 'under the flower,' and it is!"

"I bet the thief didn't know about Mama Tova's little garden behind the shop," Violet said. "But ever since Mama Tova mentioned it in the store today, now everyone knows."

"We are counting on someone who overheard us to steal the fake recipe," Henry said. "I hope the thief will think it's the real one."

"Well, we know I chose a recipe, then changed it around, adding a top-secret-thief-catching ingredient!" Jessie grinned.

"Do you think you added too much chili powder to the recipe?" Violet asked Jessie. "I wonder how it will taste."

"Nobody will want to eat a whole one," Jessie said.

"Bleech," Benny made a squished-up face. "I bet they taste gross. We will catch the thief for sure!"

A few minutes later, Grandfather knocked on the boxcar door.

"Come in," Henry called out.

Stepping inside the car, Grandfather said excitedly, "Mama Tova just called."

"Really?" Benny's eyes went wide. "What did she say?"

"Someone sneaked into her courtyard and dug up the box," Grandfather said. "The fake cupcake recipe has been stolen!"

CHAPTER 8

The Contest Begins

"There's nowhere to park," said Grandfather as he drove around the BakeMart lot. "It looks like the whole town of Greenfield turned out for the contest today."

In front of the factory, a huge white tent had been erected. Balloons, posters and colorful banners made the event look like a carnival. There was even a clown wandering around, blowing bubbles.

"I am so excited," Benny said, staring out the car window. "Oooh. There's a band playing!" Benny began bouncing up and down in his seat.

"Careful, Benny," Henry said as Grandfather pulled up in front of the tent. "You don't want to tip your tray."

"I'm being very careful." Benny had a platter full of cupcakes on his lap.

Benny was proud because he'd done most of the work to make the cupcakes by himself. "I cooked like a real chef!" he said happily, tightening his grip on the tray. "I hardly needed any help at all!"

"I know!" Jessie said, with a huge smile. "You did great."

"Thanks for the recipe," Benny said to Jessie. And to Violet he said, "I am glad you showed me how to measure ingredients."

But the biggest helper was Henry. He'd opened and closed the oven, so Benny didn't burn himself. "You're the best brother!" Benny said.

"I can't wait until Mr. Kandinsky tastes my Chocolate Surprise cupcakes." Smacking his lips together, Benny said, "I am certain he's going to love them."

The surprise in the Chocolate Surprise was all Benny's idea. After the cupcakes had cooled, Benny had cut them open and hidden a gummi worm inside each one.

"There are going to be two cupcake surprises today!" Jessie said. "Benny's sweet delicious ones, and the recipe thief's super spicy ones."

"I know we are here to catch a thief," Benny said. "But I'd also like to have my cupcakes picked as the best. That would be amazing," he admitted.

"You have a very good chance of winning," Henry told Benny as Grandfather stopped the car to let the children out.

Before driving off, Grandfather said, "The parking is so bad, I'll go pick up Mama Tova so she doesn't have to search for a space too. We will meet you inside." Henry, Jessie, Violet, and Benny headed toward the tent.

"I'll help you carry those," Jessie said to Benny as they crossed under a colorful balloon arch. But Benny refused to let go of

the tray. He wanted to bring it inside all by himself.

As they pressed through the crowd, Henry looked around. "I thought there were only nineteen names on Gretchen's list." Henry pointed a row of signs that hung above a long table. Each sign had a number. Benny's number was nineteen. Benny set down his tray under his sign.

"So, Henry, how are we going to figure out which entry is the spicy chili one?" Violet asked her brother.

Henry had thought about this and had an answer ready. "We'll have to get one cupcake from every entry and taste them ourselves."

"There are so many people at the contest," Violet said. "That's a lot of cupcakes."

Jessie glanced around the room. "It's the only way to solve this mystery!"

Benny just grinned. "I'll be happy to do the tasting part!"

"Hey look!" Jessie exclaimed.

Benny, Henry, and Violet turned to see Pauly heading towards them. He carried a large tray covered with foil.

"Hi," Pauly said, as he set the tray under the sign for Contestant Number Twenty. "I see we are going to be neighbors today."

"His name wasn't on the list," Jessie whispered to Violet, while Pauly got organized and peeled the foil off his treats. "I'm sure of that!"

Henry said, "We didn't know you were entering the BakeMart Bake-Off!"

"I wasn't going to," Pauly said. "But at the last minute, I decided to make a chocolate cupcake." He glanced at Benny's tray. "I see you made chocolate ones, too."

"Mine have a surprise in the middle," Benny said.

"That might help you score well, but really, you don't have a chance," Pauly said. "Mr. Kandinsky and the judges will like mine best."

"Why?" Violet couldn't help but ask. "What makes your cupcakes so special?"

"It runs in my family—remember, Mama Tova's my aunt," Pauly bragged. "That's what

I explained to Mr. Kandinsky when he told me it was too late to sign up. I said, 'my last name is Tova,' and he immediately agreed to give my cupcakes a try."

"I need to go tell Mr. Kandinsky I've arrived," Pauly said, after arranging his cupcakes neatly on the table. "Be right back."

As soon as Pauly walked away, Violet said, "I think that Pauly is now our new number one suspect!" Violet stared at Pauly's tray of treats. "He didn't enter the contest before, but then, very suspiciously, right after Mama Tova's 'recipe' was stolen, he joined up."

"His frosting designs sure are pretty," Jessie remarked. "And they look a lot like Mama Tova's."

"But so did Mrs. Waldman's," Henry reminded her. "Maybe Mama Tova is teaching Pauly how to decorate, too."

"There's only one way to find out if he took the fake recipe or not," Benny said. He grabbed a cupcake off of Pauly's tray and took a huge bite.

"*Paulynnotthethuf,*" he said, his mouth full.

"Chew and swallow," Henry told his brother. "Then say it again."

Benny finished his bite and then said, "Pauly isn't the thief!" He thought for a moment, then added, "They're good, but not as good as Mama Tova's. But not spicy, either."

"That means my thought about Pauly was wrong. He must have had chocolate under his fingernails," Henry said. "Not dirt from Mama Tova's planter."

"And Pauly didn't steal the recipe to sell it for baseball cards, either," Benny said.

"One down, eighteen to go," Violet announced.

"Eighteen?" Benny asked her. "But there are twenty entries."

"We already know you didn't take the recipe," Violet told him. "So you don't need to taste yours."

"Oh yeah," Benny said. He was a little sad he wasn't going to eat twenty different cupcakes today.

His mood lightened when Henry brought

over a cupcake from Contestant Number Fourteen. This would be his second tasting.

"Vanilla," Benny said, excitedly sniffing the cake. "With lemon frosting." He took a bite and made a face. "Not spicy, and not good either. This one tastes like scrambled eggs." He didn't bother to finish it.

Henry brought Benny four more cupcakes from contestants whose trays were nearby. All were yummy, but none were made from the fake recipe.

When Jessie came back from the sign-in area, she was carrying another two cupcakes behind. "I got these from Contestants Number One and Four," she said, proudly handing them to Benny.

"No," Benny said as he threw one away. "And no again," he said, eating all of the other. "That one was tasty, though. The best so far."

"Seven cupcakes down," Violet said. "Loads more to go."

That's when Henry looked over at Benny.

"I think there's a problem with this plan,"

he said. "I can't believe I didn't think of it before! Nineteen cupcakes is way too many for Benny to taste. He's already looking a little green."

"I'm not green! I can do it!" Benny insisted, patting his tummy. "There's plenty of room inside me." He looked down the line where Gretchen was busy setting up as Contestant Six, and waved at her.

"Maybe you shouldn't eat the whole thing each time," Henry suggested. "One bite should be enough to tell if there's chili powder inside or not."

"I'll only eat the yummy ones." Benny took a cupcake that Violet had brought over from Eighteen. "And I'll stop when I'm full," he promised, adding, "or when we find the thief."

Jessie made a list of numbers one through twenty in her notebook. Each time Benny tasted a cupcake, she crossed off that number if the cupcake didn't taste like chili powder.

Henry and Violet were working fast to collect one of each contestant's cupcakes before the judging began. It wasn't long before they were collecting cupcakes faster than Benny could try them. When Henry and Violet had finished gathering a sample from everyone, Benny was four cupcakes behind.

"You better hurry," Jessie said, looking down the table. "The judges are ready to start."

"I'm going fast as I can." Benny picked up the closest cupcake and took a big bite. "That was a bad one. Too gooey," Benny said, wrinkling his nose.

"Number Seven is good though," he reported after swallowing a bite of a different cupcake.

"What about Six?" Violet asked. "Did you eat that one already?"

"Six?" Benny looked at the last few cupcakes he needed to eat. "I'm about to taste it now." He peeled back the cute pink paper around a chocolate fudgy looking cupcake and took a big bite.

"I need water," Benny gasped.

Jessie handed him a bottle from her purse. "Was it spicy, Benny?" she asked as soon as Benny stopped coughing and sputtering.

"Tastes like chili," Benny said wiping his mouth with the back of his hand. "These are the cupcakes made from the fake recipe!" He didn't throw away the cupcake, however. Instead, Benny took another bite, although a much smaller one, and said, "You know, they really aren't all that bad. In fact, they are good in a different kind of way."

"That solves it, then," Jessie said, looking down into her notebook. "Now we know who stole the recipe!"

"Who?" Benny and Violet asked Jessie.

"Who made the fake recipe cupcakes?" Henry wanted to know.

Jessie looked down the table where the BakeMart judges were standing under the Number Six sign and declared, "Gretchen. Gretchen is the recipe thief."

CHAPTER 9

Mystery Solved?

As soon as Mama Tova arrived at the tent with Grandfather, the Aldens told her what they had discovered. Together they walked over to the judging table.

"What are you doing here?" Mr. Kandinsky asked Mama Tova. "If you have changed your mind about selling your cupcake recipe, it's too late." He pointed at the BakeMart judges who were talking amongst themselves in a corner. "My judges have tasted all the cupcakes and are going to announce a winner any minute now."

"I have not changed my mind," Mama Tova said, with her hands on her hips. "I am here on more important business." She looked Mr. Kandinsky right in his eyes and said, "I am here to stop a thief. One of your contestants wanted to win so badly that they tried to steal my family cupcake recipe."

Benny came to stand next to Mama Tova, saying, "We tricked the thief. She thought she was stealing Mama Tova's secret recipe, but it was really a fake."

Mr. Kandinsky's face changed. Now he looked worried. "I can't have a thief win my contest," he said. "Do you know who stole the recipe?"

"We do!" Benny told him. "Follow us."

Henry led the way across the tent. His siblings, Grandfather, Mama Tova, and Mr. Kandinsky followed. They all stopped underneath the Number Six sign.

Jessie stepped forward. "Gretchen," she said. "We need to talk to you."

Gretchen looked up at the group. She'd

been talking to Contestant Number Five and laughing about something. When she saw the group standing in front of her, her grin turned to a frown. "What's going on?" she asked.

"We know you stole Mama Tova's recipe," Henry said. He explained about the trap they'd set with the chili powder recipe.

Gretchen was confused. "Yes, there's chili powder in my recipe, but I didn't steal anything from Mama Tova." She held up her hand and vowed, "I swear."

"I tasted your cupcake and it was spicy!" Benny told her. "We invented the recipe with chili powder in it and you used it."

"It is obvious that your cupcakes were made from the fake recipe," Mama Tova said.

"My recipe is your fake recipe?" Gretchen said slowly. Then, "Oh no!" Gretchen said, lightly touching the letter *A* on the chain around her neck. "But I didn't take it!" Gretchen said.

"Really?" Henry said, considering Gretchen's statement. "You really didn't take

it?" he asked her.

"I didn't," Gretchen said. "I didn't even know the recipe was stolen. I promise—I'm not a thief!"

"Then who is?" Mama Tova asked.

Before Gretchen could answer, Violet exclaimed, "I knew there was something funny about that necklace!" Her eyes grew big as the answer came clear.

Benny and Jessie suddenly understood, too.

"A...A...A..." Benny said, pointing at Gretchen's neck.

Jessie announced, "The real thief's name begins with the letter *A*."

CHAPTER 10

Back at Mama Tova's

"Alicia!" Henry said. "She's the recipe thief."

"Alicia? Alicia, who works for me at Sweets?" Mama Tova said, surprised.

"Unfortunately, yes," Jessie said. "Alicia stole the recipe. We need to talk to her."

"It should be easy to find her." Mama Tova looked around. "Alicia told me that she'd be here today." She looked at Gretchen. "Do you know where she is?"

Gretchen had not yet let go of her necklace

and was looking very upset about everything. She shook her head then looked quickly toward the front of the tent.

"Oh, here she comes now," Violet said, as Alicia headed their way.

"Hi!" Alicia came up to where the group was standing. "I'm late. Did I miss the announcement of the winner?"

"Not yet, " Jessie said, "But…"

"Look!" Benny said. He pointed his finger at the glittery letter *G* around Alicia's neck. "Why'd you do it, Alicia?"

"Do what?" Alicia looked confused.

Benny stomped his foot. "I want to know why you tried to steal Mama Tova's secret cupcake recipe!"

Henry looked straight at Alicia and said, "We all know it was you who took the recipe from Mama Tova's garden."

Jessie explained how she'd added chili powder to the recipe so they could find the thief.

Suddenly Alicia looked scared. "I—" she began, then stopped.

A tear rolled down her face. Alicia softly touched the gold letter *G* around her neck, then started over. "I didn't mean to hurt anyone. Really. Gretchen can't afford to go to college and I was trying to help her get the money she needs." She paused to wipe away her tears.

"I was out of ideas when Mr. Kandinsky announced the contest and that there was going to be prize money." Alicia stared at her feet as she went on. "I remembered hearing Mama Tova say that the recipe was 'under the flower,' and then I realized how I could help my friend. I knew it was wrong, but Mama Tova's cupcakes are so good. Gretchen would win for sure with the recipe."

"But I don't understand why you left Sweets such a mess that first night. You could have cleaned up after you searched around for the recipe and no one would have ever known you were even looking," Jessie said.

"I was going to clean up," Alicia said. "But I didn't have enough time because I was on my way to Gretchen's birthday party and after Mrs. Waldman left, Gretchen called to say she was on her way to pick me up early."

"What about the flower box?" Henry wondered, "I bet you weren't really headed to the bookstore, were you?"

"No," Alicia admitted. "I was using the shovel to dig when you all showed up. I didn't know anyone would be coming to the shop so early. I thought I'd have enough time to search in the flowerbox and clean it up before anyone came to Sweets."

Gretchen then turned to Alicia and said, "You told me the recipe was your mom's. I would have never used it if I knew you'd stolen it!"

A fresh tear rolled down Alicia's cheek. "I am so sorry I lied to you."

Jessie shut her notebook, saying, "Stealing is a bad thing to do, even if you were doing it for a good reason, Alicia."

"I know," Alicia said, hanging her head. "I'll do whatever it takes to make things right," Alicia looked at Mama Tova through her tears.

While Mama Tova thought about what to do, Mr. Kandinsky spoke up.

"Jessie told me everything and I have an idea of how Alicia can make up for the trouble she's caused," he said. "Mama Tova, can I talk to you?" Mr. Kandinsky looked around at everyone and added, "In private?"

"I'd like to hear your idea," Mama Tova said.

The two of them stepped aside and when they returned a few minutes later, Mama Tova announced, "Alicia can make up for the trouble she's caused by helping Mr. Kandinsky with his new cupcake business."

"Really?" Alicia asked, looking up at Mr. Kandinsky. "How?"

"It's not going to be an easy job," Mr. Kandinsky said. "You are going to clean up the factory every evening after the cupcakes are made. It seems the fairest punishment for the mess you made at Mama Tova's."

"You can't work at Sweets again," Mama Tova told Alicia. Then, she stepped closer to

Mr. Kandinsky. "But I think working at the factory is a good idea."

"I promise I'll make the factory shine. I'll be the hardest worker you ever had," Alicia told Mr. Kandinsky, who smiled slightly, making the corners of his moustache rise.

"I don't understand. Why are you letting Mr. Kandinsky decide Alicia's punishment?" Jessie asked Mama Tova. "Aren't you mad at him? He wanted to put you out of business."

"From now on, Mama Tova and I are going to be friends. I want Mama Tova and her shop to stay just the way they are," Mr. Kandinsky explained. "Instead of sweet dessert cupcakes, like Mama Tova's, BakeMart is going to make spicy ones to be eaten with dinner!"

"Spicy?" Henry said.

Mr. Kandinsky pulled a blue first place ribbon out of his pocket and pinned it on Gretchen's shirt. "Your unique cupcakes won the contest."

He straightened the ribbon then added, "We are going to put a little less chili powder in the final recipe, cut down the sugar, then I think that we can sell them to every restaurant in town. They'd be great with chicken, or steak, or Mexican food. The possibilities are endless."

Gretchen took the ribbon off her shirt and handed it to Jessie saying, "Mr. Kandinsky, Jessie made up that recipe. I didn't. The prize money should be hers."

"No thanks," Jessie gave the ribbon back to Gretchen. "Take the money. You need it. I have a long time before I'm going to college."

"Really?" Gretchen asked. "You really mean it?" After Jessie nodded, Gretchen took back the first place bow and shook hands with Jessie. "Thanks."

As the Alden children were preparing to leave the shop and head back home, Mr. Kandinsky stopped Benny. "How did you happen to taste Gretchen's cupcake?" Mr. Kandinsky asked. "Only the judges were allowed to eat the cupcakes."

Benny shrugged. "Honestly, I tasted them all." He quickly added, "I had to. It was the only way we could find the thief."

Mr. Kandinsky nodded, asking "And?"

"And what?" Benny asked, a little afraid he was in trouble for sneaking cupcakes.

Mr. Kandinsky wasn't upset. He broke into a slow smile, asking, "Which one did you like the best?" Mr. Kandinsky pressed. "Which would you pick? Would it have been yours? Pauly's? Which ones?"

Benny considered it a moment and said, "All the cupcakes at the contest are second place to Mama Tova's."

"That's just what I thought, too," Mr. Kandinsky said, patting Benny on the head. "That's why I decided it would be better to change the way we at BakeMart think about cupcakes."

"Cupcakes for dinner," Benny said, grinning big. "That's the best idea I've ever heard!"

*   *   *

In the boxcar later that night, Benny had an important question to ask. "Jessie," he said

to his sister as she worked on her laptop. "What's sasparilla?"

"I'm not sure," Jessie said. "I'll look it up." She opened up a new web page.

"Why do you want to know?" Violet said. She looked up from the book she'd been reading.

Benny replied, "There were all those crates of it in Mama Tova's kitchen. I don't know what it is."

"The crates you were jumping off of?" Henry asked.

"Yes," Benny replied. "I was wondering what was inside those."

"Sasparilla," Jessie read from the internet. "It's root beer."

"Delicious," Benny said. "But Mama Tova only serves milk and lemonade to drink. Why does she have all that root beer in her kitchen?"

"Do you think root beer could be the secret ingredient in Mama Tova's cupcakes?" Jessie asked, swirling quickly around in her chair.

"The crates were right under the bags of

flour on the shelf. Under the flower…under the flour…" Henry said. "We might have figured out more than one mystery today."

"We'll never know for sure," Jessie said.

"But just in case we're right, we better keep this one quiet," Violet added.

Even though he trusted his siblings, Benny made everyone pinky promise not to tell.

They all linked pinkies in a circle in the middle of the boxcar, and Benny declared, "Jessie, Henry, Violet and me—we are the protectors of Mama Tova's secret. For now and ever more."

They all shook fingers.